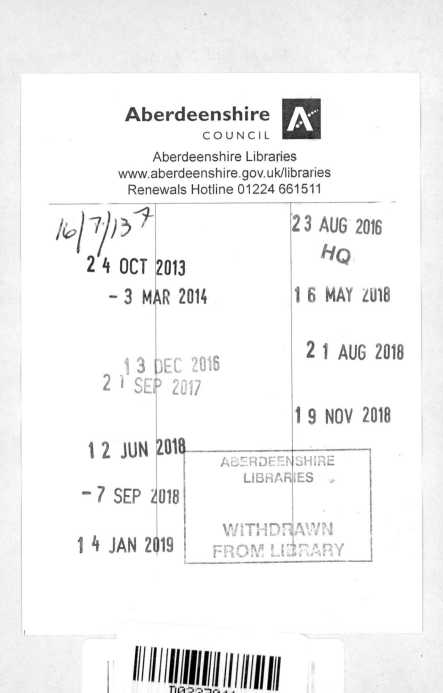

Also by Sally Grindley

Paw Prints in the Snow
Shadows under the Sea
Feathers in the Wind

My Name Is Rose
Bitter Chocolate
Torn Pages
Broken Glass
Spilled Water
Saving Finnegan
Hurricane Wills
Feather Wars

Danger
in the
Dust

Sally Grindley

BLOOMSBURY

LONDON NEW DELHI NEW YORK SYDNEY

Bloomsbury Publishing, London, New Delhi, New York and Sydney

First published in Great Britain in July 2013 by Bloomsbury Publishing Plc
50 Bedford Square, London WC1B 3DP

Manufactured and supplied under licence from the Zoological Society of London

Licensed by Bright Group International
www.thebrightagency.com

With thanks to ZSL's conservation team

A CIP catalogue record for this book is available from the British Library

ISBN 978 1 4088 1946 3

MIX
Paper from
responsible sources
FSC® C020471
FSC
www.fsc.org

Typeset by Hewer Text UK Ltd, Edinburgh
Printed and bound in Great Britain by CPI Group (UK) Ltd, Croydon CR0 4YY

1 3 5 7 9 10 8 6 4 2

www.storiesfromthezoo.com
www.bloomsbury.com
www.sallygrindley.co.uk

For Watlington Primary School
in Oxfordshire

Chapter 1

'Can you believe that the number of black rhinos in Kenya fell from 20,000 to only 381 between the 1970s and 1990s?'

Peter Brook watched for his family's reaction as they sat around the kitchen table after enjoying a late Sunday breakfast. He had just told his children, Joe and Aesha, that they would be spending their Easter holidays in East Africa, where he had been asked to photograph the release of black rhinos back into the wild in Kenya.

'That's awful, Dad!' said Aesha, whose reaction

changed from excitement at the prospect of going to Africa to shock at the dramatic decline in the rhino population. 'Why?'

'It's mostly because of poaching,' Binti, her mother, replied. 'Rhino horn is prized in some societies for its apparent healing properties.'

Joe was indignant. 'I can't believe rhinos are being killed because some people think their horns will heal them.'

'Poachers make a lot of money from selling the horn,' Peter explained.

'The outlook for rhinos is better than it was, and their numbers are increasing,' said Binti. 'The fact that some rhinos are being released back into the wild is a success story. They've been confined to fenced sanctuaries and moni-tored there, but it was always the aim to return them to their former homes, provided it was safe to do so.'

'But won't the poachers kill the rhinos that are released?' Joe asked.

'Wherever rhinos are, they're never one

hundred per cent safe, even in the sanctuaries,' Binti replied. 'But there are many more anti-poaching patrols operating now and poachers are dealt with much more harshly. Everyone is praying that the released rhinos won't just survive but will thrive.'

'Baby rhinos are cute,' said Joe. 'And the adults are cool too. I think it's because they look sort of prehistoric – like dinosaurs.'

'They look grumpy to me,' observed Aesha. 'I prefer elephants. Will we be able to see elephants when we're in Africa?'

'If my princess wants to see elephants, then elephants she shall see,' said Peter. 'I'll have them line up and trumpet for you.'

'That's not very funny, Dad.' Aesha groaned.

'Are we going on safari?' Joe asked excitedly.

'Absolutely!' said Binti. 'And we'll be going to Tanzania to visit my family as well!'

'Whoopee!' said Joe.

He had met his maternal grandparents, aunts, uncles and cousins twice before, once when he was still a baby, and the second time when they had spent ten days in Tanzania three years ago when he was six. It was difficult for them to visit more often, because Tanzania was so far away and because his parents' hectic work schedules left them with very little spare time. Peter was a wildlife photographer and Binti was an international vet, both of them in demand to work on conservation projects all over the world.

Once in a while, Binti would sigh wistfully and say how much she missed her homeland. 'I love my life in England, but I loved my life back home as well, especially the animals and the wide open spaces.'

Joe remembered the swathes of grassland and the dusty roads and bustling towns, with Mount Kilimanjaro in the background, its peak capped with snow. They hadn't gone on safari last time they were there because he was too young. Now he couldn't wait for what he was sure would be a big adventure.

'Will we be allowed to watch when they release the rhinos?' he asked his father, who had just stood up from the table to rifle through the Sunday papers.

'That I don't know,' said Peter. 'Rhinos are dangerous animals when they're upset – a bit like your mum when she gets out of the wrong side of the bed – and they might be upset after a bumpy trip confined in a truck.'

'Cheeky!' said Binti, standing up as well. 'But if you want a dangerous animal, you shall have one. I don't know how many times I've asked you all to tidy the garage, but if it isn't done soon we won't be going anywhere because I can't even get to the suitcases! I think you should make that your project for today.'

'Watch out, you two – your mum's about to go on the rampage! I think you'd better do as she says,' Peter urged, cowering melodramatically behind a cupboard door.

'You too, Dad!' exclaimed Aesha. 'There's loads of your stuff in there.'

'My "stuff", as you call it, is the essential equipment of a highly regarded, not to mention highly sought-after, expert in the field of photography,' her father replied haughtily.

'It's still essentially in the way,' Aesha retorted. 'You can't expect us to be tidy when you're not. You've probably given us an untidiness gene.'

'The state of the garage has nothing to do with genetics,' Binti declared. 'Now, off with you – all of you – before my rhino gene really kicks in.'

'Quick!' squealed Joe. 'She's coming after us. Help!'

Chapter 2

Joe enjoyed tidying the garage, much to his surprise. He came across toys and games he'd forgotten about, two of which he decided to reinstate in his bedroom.

When his father found a box of photographs from their trip to the Philippines, they sat together on an upturned crate, going through them and recalling where they had been taken.

'We're supposed to be clearing up, not reminiscing,' Aesha grumbled, though she kept stopping to look over their shoulders and her own efforts were somewhat half-hearted.

'There's a lovely picture of you here,' Peter said, grinning and showing it to her.

'That snorkel mask really suits you.' Joe laughed.

Aesha snatched the photograph and tore it up.

'You're mean,' she said. 'Anyway, Dad, you look like a pot-bellied pig in that one.'

She pointed to a photograph Joe had taken of their father in his swimming shorts holding up a bunch of seaweed.

'I do not!' Peter protested hotly. 'That finely honed body could model for any number of top magazines, if only someone would discover it.'

'Yeah, wildlife magazines!' Joe hooted. 'We could take photos of you posing with an elephant and ask people to spot the difference!'

'I have such cruel children.' Peter sighed. 'Nobody understands what I have to put up with.'

There was a sudden barking at the door. Joe jumped up and opened it to Foggy, the family schnauzer, who made his way straight to Peter and put his head on his master's knee.

'Nobody except Foggy,' Peter added, stroking his ears.

'I don't know why he likes you when you're the one who sticks him in the doggery every time we go away,' said Aesha.

'Waggy Tails Boarding Kennels is the equivalent of a five-star hotel but for dogs,' Peter countered. 'He'll be treated like a superstar while he's there.'

'Do they treat animals well in zoos?' Joe asked.

'Good zoos do,' said Peter. 'When I went to London Zoo to take photos for a magazine project, I was shown to a meal preparation room where the walls were covered with menu boards for each species, with special diets for the elderly and sick – including one for a gibbon with no teeth! Not only that, but the meat and vegetables were top quality. There was even a shelf lined with large jars full of spices so that the keepers could add variety to the animals' meals. In fact, I thought about moving in!'

'Cool!' said Joe. 'Can we go in there one day?'

'You'll have to ask your mother to arrange it,' Peter replied. 'But the answer will be a big no if we don't get a move on with this garage.'

He stood up and gently pushed Foggy back out through the door.

'Do you think we'll see leopards when we're on safari?' Joe asked, as he repositioned his bike so that it wasn't blocking his mother's filing cabinet.

'It's not very likely,' Aesha piped up. 'Leopards are extremely rare and they're very well camouflaged.'

'You'd think their spots would make them easy to see, wouldn't you?' Joe said thoughtfully.

'Shadows make trees and grass appear dappled, which plays tricks with your eyes, and that's why leopards and cheetahs are hard to pick out with their spotted coats,' Peter explained. 'But the safari guides know where they're most likely to be sighted, so we might be lucky.'

'It would be so cool to be a safari guide,' said Joe. 'Can you imagine spending all day tracking animals in the wild and watching them hunting and playing?'

'I bet it would soon get boring,' Aesha responded.

'I don't think it would get boring at all,' Joe said hotly. 'It's nowhere near as boring as working in an office, is it, Dad? Is this tidy enough now?'

'I think it should just about pass your mother's high standards,' Peter said, picking up two large suitcases and signalling for Aesha to open the door.

Foggy, who had stationed himself on sentry duty on the other side, leapt to his feet the moment he saw them and looked up, as though expecting some sort of treat for his dedication.

'All done?' Binti enquired, when they walked back into the house.

'It's spick, span and spotless,' Peter assured her.

Joe disappeared up to his bedroom, in case his mother had any other chores for him. He wanted to immerse himself in a book about African wildlife that he had found on her book-case. He knew about 'the Big Five' – elephants, rhinos, lions, leopards and buffaloes – and that they would see zebras, wildebeests and lots of different antelopes, but he was keen to find out if there were any lesser known animals that he could keep a lookout for.

Stretching out on his bed, he was thrilled to read that he might see hippos, and giggled at a photograph of a group of them wallowing in a muddy river. He wondered if there were croco-diles as well.

It would be so cool to see a crocodile, he thought to himself. *Crocodiles must be the scariest animals ever!*

What surprised Joe most was the discovery that ostriches live on the savannah, and he hadn't realised they were so big until he came to a photograph of one standing close to a giraffe.

'I hope we see an ostrich and a cheetah and a leopard and a crocodile and a hippo,' he said to Peter, who had poked his head round the bedroom door to ask if he wanted to go to the shops with him.

'I don't think Surrey is renowned for its wildlife!' Peter said, chuckling loudly.

It seemed no time at all between the day they retrieved their suitcases from the garage and the day before their departure, when Joe carefully cushioned his camera in the middle of his case. In just a few hours they would be on their way to Kenya and a whole new world of adventure would open up before them. Joe was certain that this would turn out to be one of their best trips ever, especially since there were so many animals to be spotted. He had checked his camera over and cleaned the lenses, taking special care with the long-distance lens his father had bought him for their trip to India, where they had helped with vulture conservation.

I'll definitely need that. He grinned. *I definitely won't be taking close-up shots of a rhino!*

Joe hoped to follow in his father's footsteps as a wildlife photographer, though sometimes he thought he would prefer to be a vet like his mother. Either way, he wanted to be involved with helping animals. His friend Adam had told him he was the luckiest boy in their school because his parents' professions gave him the opportunity to go to such amazing places. Joe couldn't help but agree. In the past few months he and his family had been to eastern Russia, the Philippines and India. Now they were about to go to East Africa.

On the last day of school it seemed no one wanted to talk about anything else! Everyone asked Joe about the animals he was going to see. They even devised a rowdy game where they charged around the school field in teams,

some of them rhinos and some of them elephants, and the winning team was the one to
knock over the most opponents. It made Joe
feel important, even though he was on the
losing team of elephants and had a number of
bruises to show for it.

'All my friends wish they were going to
Africa with me,' he said to Binti on the way
home. 'Can one of them come with us one
day?'

'I think you and Aesha get into more than
enough scrapes when it's just the two of you!'
she replied.

'I promise not to get into any scrapes this
time,' he said.

'I don't think you can help yourself!' Binti
laughed. 'You seem to attract trouble.'

Chapter 3

The next day, when they were boarding the flight to Kenya, Joe was so excited he didn't give a second's thought to the friends he was leaving behind. His new adventure was just beginning and he didn't want to miss a moment of it. He was used to flying now and enjoyed the routine of drinks and meals, reading and watching films, sleeping and observing his fellow passengers.

Across the aisle from him, a young man with dark hair, and wearing jeans and a crumpled shirt, was making himself comfortable, tightening his seat belt and plumping up the meagre pillow he had been given to put behind his head. He shifted from side to side, trying to find the best position for his long legs, and returned Joe's gaze.

'There's never enough room for tall people,' he observed. 'It's a pity I can't take my legs off and hang them up somewhere.'

Joe grinned shyly. 'An overhead locker full of passengers' legs would be funny,' he said.

'Especially if I took the wrong ones at the end of the flight,' the man replied, laughing loudly.

Joe wondered why he was going to Kenya and what he would do when he was there.

'Are you going on safari?' the man asked him.

Joe nodded. 'And we're going to help release some rhinos into the wild,' he added importantly.

'Are you indeed?' The man looked very impressed and leant towards him. 'Tell me more. I'm fascinated by the subject – by anything to do with conservation, in fact. Where are they being released?'

Joe bit his lip, all of a sudden unsure whether

he should have mentioned the rhinos in case this man had anything to do with poaching.

'I can't remember the name of the place,' he said quietly. 'You'll have to ask my dad. He's going to be photographing them, but I don't know where and when, and I don't think anyone else will be allowed to be there because rhinos are very dangerous.'

Joe ended the conversation by looking away and opening his book, before scolding himself inwardly for imagining that the man was anything other than an innocent fellow traveller. He knew his father would laugh at him if he voiced any suspicions, because on their way to Russia Joe had decided, wrongly, that one of the plane's passengers was a smuggler of tiger parts. Peter had teased him about it ever since.

But what if I'm right this time? Joe wondered. *Why does that man want to know where the rhinos are being released?*

The words danced on the pages of his book and refused to make sense. He felt hot and uncomfortable. His parents hadn't told him not to say anything about the release of the rhinos, but he was convinced that one word spoken casually to the wrong person could put them in danger. He would have to tell them if he saw the man following them once they arrived in Kenya.

Joe was relieved when the man fell asleep after they had eaten their in-flight meal.

'Is it a secret where the rhinos are being released?' he whispered to his mother.

'It's not necessarily a secret, but I don't think anyone will be broadcasting the location either.' Binti looked at him quizzically. 'It's not as if it'll be anywhere accessible to the general public.'

'How will they get the rhinos to the place where they're going to be released?' Joe asked.

'They put them into large crates and drive them there,' said Binti.

'I bet the rhinos don't like that!' Joe could just imagine them stamping their feet and pushing against the sides of the crates.

'No, I don't suppose they do.' Binti smiled at him.

'How do they get the rhinos into the crates?'

'It must take many men, a lot of ropes and a good deal of patience,' said Binti.

Joe cast a quick glance at the man opposite and whispered, 'No one would be able to ambush the drivers before they reached the reserve, would they?'

Even as he said this he realised how ridiculous it was going to sound to his mother.

'You're letting your imagination run away with you,' Binti said, smiling.

'I just want the rhinos to be safe, that's all,' said Joe.

He was impatient now for the flight to end so that he could get away from the man and the silly thoughts he had had about him. He leant against his mother's shoulder and closed his eyes.

When Joe opened his eyes again, he was pleased to hear they would soon be landing in Nairobi.

'I expect you're excited, aren't you?' said his neighbour from across the aisle. 'I know I would be if I were in your shoes.'

Joe tried to smile at him.

'Maybe I'll bump into you guys while I'm in Kenya,' the man continued.

'We're not staying in Kenya all the time,' Joe said quickly. 'We're going to Tanzania as well.'

'Then you're one very lucky boy,' the man said, before turning to chat with the woman on the other side of him.

Joe wished his parents had been able to choose window seats so that he could watch the plane coming in to land, but because there were four of them they often wound up in the middle rows on larger aircraft. He tried to see past his family to the window on the far side, but all that was visible was a small square of blue.

'Are you OK, Joe?' Peter asked him. 'You look a bit glum.'

Before Joe could answer, the plane's engines

began to roar, there was a series of loud clunks, and a few seconds later a hefty bump shook the whole fuselage, followed by another. The engines screamed and Joe felt himself being pushed back in his seat, until at last the plane slowed enough for him to be able to relax.

'That wasn't the smoothest landing,' his father said cheerily.

'The pilot should have to take his test again,' said Aesha, pursing her lips.

'Shall I go and tell him?' Peter offered.

Aesha glared at him. 'You're not funny, Dad.'

Peter put his arm round her. 'Sorry, darling. I must try harder.'

'I thought we were going to crash-land!' said Joe.

The plane taxied to a halt and everyone jumped to their feet. Joe waited until his neighbour had moved forward down the aisle before standing up. Now he could really enjoy the start of the trip.

'How long till we go on safari?' he asked his mother, as they waited to disembark.

'We'll spend this evening and tomorrow morning in Nairobi, then set off for the Maasai Mara after lunch,' said Binti. 'There's somewhere in Nairobi I want us to visit before we leave.'

She wouldn't tell Joe where, but assured him he would like it. He and Aesha tried to find out more during the taxi ride to the hotel, but their parents stubbornly refused to provide even the slightest clue.

'One thing at a time,' said Peter. 'First you need to shower and change into some fresh clothes, because this evening we're going somewhere very, very special to eat. As for tomorrow – tomorrow is another day.'

Chapter 4

The special place to eat was a big open-air restaurant where they served every variety of meat, including ostrich, crocodile and zebra. Joe couldn't believe his eyes when they walked in. There was a huge charcoal pit just inside the entrance, into which numerous waiters thrust long skewers covered with meat, withdrawing them when the meat was cooked and carrying them to the eager diners.

'Those skewers are traditional Maasai warrior swords,' said Peter, as they were shown to their table.

'Are we really going to eat crocodile?' Joe was incredulous.

'I'm not!' said Aesha. 'And I'm not going to eat ostrich or zebra, either.'

'But that's why people come here — to try something different,' Peter said. 'You won't find endangered species on the menu, and the amount of wild meat on offer is very carefully controlled.'

'I don't care,' said Aesha. 'It doesn't seem right to eat it when we've come all this way to see these animals alive.'

'I suppose it's no different from eating lamb or chicken,' Joe mused, though he wasn't sure he liked the idea of crocodile, which he guessed would be tough. 'I would never eat elephant or rhino, or leopard or giraffe, though,' he added.

'And yet if they were plentiful and tasted good, there'd be no real reason not to,' Binti replied.

Aesha pulled a face. 'I'm going to have the vegetarian option,' she said stubbornly.

'That's fine,' said Binti. 'The salads and vegetables look wonderful too.'

One by one, the waiters came to serve them, each carrying a sword loaded with a single meat. Joe watched with fascination as they held the swords, pointed end down, and carved slices of the different meats on to his sizzling, cast-iron plate. To start with there was beef, lamb and spare ribs. Next came chicken wings and sirloin steak.

'Tuck in,' Peter encouraged. 'There's plenty more to come.'

Joe tried each of the meats in turn. He had never tasted anything quite so good, even though his father was a brilliant cook. When the sword laden with ostrich arrived, he hesitated at first, then asked for just a small piece. It was so delicious, however, he couldn't wait for the waiter to return with more.

'The waiters will keep coming back to top up our plates until we take down that little white flag in the middle of the table,' Peter explained. 'That's how we let them know we're full.'

'I'm full now!' declared Aesha, who was working her way through a platter piled high with salads and cheeses.

'No room for crocodile?' Peter asked.

'I'm surprised you didn't say anything about making it snappy,' Aesha said scornfully.

'Here's the crocodile now,' said Binti, as a waiter approached carrying a sword covered with small circles of pale-coloured meat.

Joe allowed him to slide two pieces on to his plate.

'It doesn't look how I imagined it would,' he remarked, staring dubiously at the two pieces. He tasted one of them, but pushed the other aside. 'Too chewy,' he said, and contented himself with a jumbo sausage that had also appeared on his plate.

Shortly after, he joined Aesha in deciding that he was too full to eat another thing.

'I feel like an elephant,' Aesha grumbled.

'They don't serve it here,' said Peter, which earned him a prolonged scowl.

'Do you think it's right that we sit here, eating mountains of food, in a continent where some people are starving?' Aesha asked bluntly.

'That's a difficult one,' said Binti. 'It's never "right" that some people have plenty while others starve. But our custom here will help put food on the tables of families who might otherwise go without, and this is a one-off evening of indulgence.'

Despite his parents' reassurances, Joe felt uncomfortable now with the heap of undigested meat sitting in his stomach. Tiredness was overwhelming him and all he wanted to do was go back to their hotel and sleep.

The moment the bill had been paid, he struggled to his feet and leant against his mother for support.

'Someone's had enough,' she said, stroking his hair. 'We'd better get you to bed or you won't have any energy for tomorrow's treat.'

'Which is?' Aesha jumped in, hoping to catch her mother out.

'Which is for you to find out tomorrow,' Binti said, smiling.

As soon as they returned to the hotel, Joe fell into bed and snuggled down under the crisp white sheets. It was hard to believe that only that morning he had woken up in his own bed, eager for their journey to begin. Now, here he was in Africa, listening to the unfamiliar sounds of the Nairobi night and reliving the events of the day.

He began to mull over their evening in the restaurant. The one thing he couldn't get out of his mind was the fact that one of the animals he had most wanted to see was an ostrich, and yet he had eaten ostrich meat before he had even seen a real, live one! He wasn't sure he liked that idea very much, but reminded himself that he would quite happily eat beef and watch young calves at play in the same day.

If I decide to be a vet, I'll have to cope with things like that all the time, he thought.

Deciding he would prefer to follow in his father's footsteps, he fell asleep.

Chapter 5

Joe was overjoyed when, the next morning, Binti announced that they were going to visit an elephant orphanage.

'There's only a one-hour viewing slot, so we mustn't be late,' she said.

'Will there be any calves? And will we be able to get close to them?' Joe wanted to know as they set off from the hotel.

'There might be one or two very young calves, but most will be older, I believe,' Binti replied. 'I'm sure I can arrange for us to see them close up.'

'That's the advantage of having an international vet for a mother,' said Peter. 'She can open many doors that would otherwise be out of bounds.'

Joe held his camera case tightly as they waited for their taxi to arrive to take them to the orphanage, which was located on the outskirts of Nairobi.

It was a beautiful morning, though it had rained heavily during the night, and Joe was surprised at how green everything was. He had assumed that the landscape would be parched and dusty, and was surprised, too, at all the high-rise buildings that broke up the skyline.

'Nairobi is like a lot of cities, isn't it?' he said.

'Yeah, it's very noisy,' said Aesha.

'I didn't expect it to be so sort of . . . modern,' he added.

'It's a big melting pot,' said Peter. 'It's a real mix of skyscrapers, restaurants, cafés, shops and offices, parks and gardens, a number of very affluent housing complexes, and there are also the most appalling slums, where about half the city's population lives. But Nairobi really stands out from other cities in that it has a national park right on its doorstep. Nairobi National Park is home to four of the Big Five, as well as numerous other animals and birds.'

'Cool!' exclaimed Joe. 'Can we go there?'

'The orphanage is just on the border of the park,' said Binti. 'You might see some animals while we're there, but we're saving most of our game viewing till we go on safari.'

Joe pulled a face. He would have been quite happy to see wild animals every hour and minute of their trip.

He didn't have to wait long. As the taxi took them towards their destination, the driver told them to look to their right. To Joe's amazement, there was a giraffe striding across a wide open space towards a clump of low-growing trees, with the cityscape in the background.

'Wow!' cried Aesha. 'You just wouldn't expect to see a giraffe so close to houses!

Imagine looking out of your bedroom window and being able to see a wild animal like that!'

I'd love to live here, Joe thought. *I can't imagine anything more exciting than having wild animals roaming right outside your window.*

He kept his eyes peeled for the rest of the journey, hoping to see more animals, but soon the taxi driver pulled up outside some gates and told them that they had arrived. They piled out of the car and joined the queue to get into the orphanage. Joe looked at his watch. It was a quarter to eleven. He didn't want to miss one second of his time with the elephants and willed the gates to open.

An official came to the entrance and ushered them through. They were shepherded to an expanse of scrubby ground dotted with small trees, which stretched away into the distant horizon.

A large area close by was cordoned off with rope along one side and an official asked the group of spectators to stand behind it.

'What do you think is going to happen?' whispered Joe to his mother. 'Where are the elephants?'

'Wait and see.' Binti smiled at him.

'You'd better get your camera out, Joe,' Peter said, adjusting the lens on his video camera. 'You won't want to miss this.'

Joe took his camera from its case and held it at the ready. Several keepers in green overalls spilled out from the orphanage building, one of them kicking a football, another pulling a cart loaded with feeding bottles. Joe expected the elephants to appear from somewhere behind them, but suddenly a keeper pointed in the direction of the park.

'They are coming,' the keeper announced.

All Joe could see at first was another man in green overalls. Then he spotted a small browny-grey shape trundling along after him.

'Oh, look!' cried Aesha. 'It's a baby, and there's a bigger one following it!'

'I can see three now!' cried Joe. 'Four!'

Altogether, there were nine elephants in the procession. As they came closer, a spokesperson informed the crowd that the youngest was only three months old and that his mother had been shot by poachers. The same fate had met the mothers of five of the other calves, while two calves had been rescued from wells and the final one had been orphaned when his mother died from illness.

As the elephants reached the roped-off area, the keepers each took a bottle of milk and chose an elephant to feed. Joe could hardly contain his excitement – he was almost able to touch them and one was being given its bottle right in front of him.

'We feed them every three hours, day and night, just like their mothers would,' said the spokesperson. 'And we sleep with them too, one keeper to each elephant, though we swap around so that they don't become too attached to a particular individual.'

The bottles were finished in no time and

several of the elephants headed for a large pool of muddy water, running into it and splashing around, much to the delight of the crowd. Two of the keepers started to kick the football to each other, encouraging the elephants to join in. Joe couldn't help laughing when one of the smaller elephants stopped the ball with one foot then kicked it away with another, before hurtling after it and trying to swipe it with its trunk.

'That's a big advantage, having four feet and a trunk to use,' said Peter.

It wasn't such an advantage for one calf, which got the ball caught between its back legs and sat down on it. Meanwhile, the elephants in the pool were lumbering backwards and forwards and squirting each other with water from their trunks. The youngest tried to clamber out, found the sides too high and slid back in on its tummy, bumping into another that was standing behind it and knocking it off its feet.

'They're hilarious!' Aesha was entranced.

Joe thought it was one of the best hours he

had ever spent and took one photograph after another. All too quickly, though, the fun and games were over, as the elephants were led back into the park for the afternoon and the crowd was asked to leave. Joe turned to follow everyone else, but just then the spokesperson called his and Aesha's names and signalled for them to go with him. Joe looked questioningly at his father, who shrugged his shoulders and told him to blame his mother.

They soon found themselves standing in front of an enclosure containing two goats and the orphanage's most recent arrival – a two-month-old rhino calf, whose mother had been shot by poachers.

'It's so cute! I told you baby rhinos are cute,' he said to Aesha. 'What's its name?' he asked the keeper.

'His name is Rombo,' the keeper replied.

To Joe and Aesha's delight, they were invited to take it in turns feeding Rombo from a large bottle with a teat on the end.

'He hasn't quite got the idea that there's something good for him in the bottle, so squirt the milk at his mouth until he tastes it and works out where it's coming from,' the keeper suggested.

Joe did as he was told, spraying the milk until Rombo turned towards him and, with a bit of help from the keeper, latched on to the teat.

'If this little chap's mother hadn't been killed, he would have stayed with her for the first two to three years of his life. She would have taught him everything he needed to know to survive.'

'Poor Rombo,' said Aesha.

Joe studied the thick grey hide of the calf and the bump on his nose that would become his horn.

'His ears look like trumpets,' he said.

'Those ears are perfect for hearing,' said the keeper, 'which is just as well, because those little eyes are very short-sighted.'

Rombo finished his milk in no time and trundled away to harass the goats.

'He is very happy that you have decided to adopt him.' Rombo's keeper grinned at Aesha and Joe, and winked at Binti.

'From now on, we'll be paying for his upkeep and the orphanage will send us news about his progress every month,' said Binti.

Joe was thrilled. 'That's so cool!'

Chapter 6

The rest of the day, after the Brook family had left the orphanage and collected their suitcases from the hotel, was spent travelling from Nairobi to the Maasai Mara National Reserve. The journey took several hours in a four-wheel drive, along roads pitted with deep holes and slippery with mud from the pouring rain. Joe slept much of the time, waking only to wonder if the rain would ever stop and to marvel that they were able to keep going on a road that presented so many challenges.

By the time they reached the Maasai Mara, darkness had fallen. Peter told them that they were going to stay on a campsite just inside the border of the reserve, rather than in a hotel. Aesha groaned loudly, but Joe couldn't imagine anything better.

'Are we really going to be sleeping in a tent? Will there be wild animals close by?' he asked.

'It's very likely we'll hear animals in the night, but they don't normally come into the camps,' Binti assured him, presuming he had asked because he was worried.

'I think it would be amazing to have wild animals prowling around,' said Joe.

Aesha snorted. 'You wouldn't think it was amazing if one came into the tent.'

'There's not much chance of that,' said Peter. 'The camps are patrolled by rangers.'

The tents were much bigger than Joe had expected and he was pleased to hear he would be sharing one with his father.

'You'd better not snore!' he warned him.

'For someone who likes the idea of wild animals prowling around, I don't think my snoring will cause much disturbance,' Peter responded.

After they'd eaten a hearty meal with another group of travellers and shared stories round a campfire, they returned to their tents for the night. Joe tried to make himself comfortable on his hard bed with its thin pillow and listened to the noises that drifted in from outside, trying to identify the sounds of animals beyond the human voices and movements.

Joe must have fallen asleep, because the next thing he was aware of was the low rumble of his father's snoring and, apart from that, nothing but silence. He was bursting to go to the loo! The toilets were a short walk away and Binti had told him it was perfectly safe to go in the night, but Joe lay there for some time, reluctant to venture out.

'You won't catch me leaving my tent in the night, patrol or no patrol!' Aesha had said.

Joe wondered about waking his father and

asking him to go with him. He leant over and half-heartedly touched his shoulder. His father snorted loudly, turned over and stopped snoring. The new silence was worse than the snoring – it made Joe feel completely alone.

Don't be such a wimp! he scolded himself.

With that he clambered out of bed and tried to find the torch his father had left on the floor between them. He couldn't find it anywhere. He fumbled his way towards the tent opening and pushed his way out. It was pitch black everywhere. The lights that had lit the pathways earlier had been turned off. He thought he knew which way to go, but in the darkness doubts crept in. He contemplated peeing on the ground behind the tent, but worried about tripping over the guy ropes or being caught out by a ranger.

Joe couldn't wait any longer – he was desperate! He turned left, away from the tent, and walked slowly along what he hoped was the path, putting one foot carefully in front of the other. A thin shaft of moonlight illuminated what looked to him like the toilet block, but it quickly disappeared at the same time as drops of rain began to fall.

Oh no! I'll get soaked!

He walked faster, the torrential rain that was thudding to the ground disorientating him. He was no longer sure he was heading in the right direction and, as he considered giving up and going back, he heard a series of ghostly wails from somewhere close by. He panicked and started to run, the rain filling his eyes and soaking his T-shirt.

'Mum, Dad, where are you?' he shouted.

His flight came to an end when he hit something soft and solid – and screamed.

'Shhh. It's all right, boy. You'll wake everyone up.'

A man's voice – calm, taking control. Joe stared through the darkness, but all he could see were the whites of the man's eyes.

'Where were you going, boy?'

Joe gulped in air to try and steady his nerves. 'To the toilet,' he said weakly. 'I heard something howling.'

'Those were jackals you heard. Don't worry – they're outside the camp. The toilets are this way.'

Joe hesitated for a second, before following the man, who told him his name was Kwame and that he was a night patrolman. Joe was so relieved when Kwame led him to the toilet block, switched on the light and waited for him.

Kwame then showed him the way back to the tent, which was no distance at all, and told him that the heavy rain would make the early-morning safaris much trickier.

'Your guide may have to stay on the roads if the ground is too wet, but they like to go off-road if they can.'

'Does that mean we won't see as many animals?' asked Joe.

'Maybe,' said Kwame.

He wished Joe goodnight and walked away.

Joe tiptoed into the tent, took off his wet clothes and got back into bed. He lay there shivering for a while; from the chill air, from his earlier fright, and from anxiety that because of the rain they might miss out on some of the animals he had set his heart on seeing.

'Please stop raining,' he muttered, as he listened to it hammering down.

Chapter 7

Joe was woken the next morning by Peter's hand on his shoulder.

'Wake up, sleepyhead. We're going on an early-morning safari. It's the best time to see lots of animals.'

It took Joe a moment to take in what his father was saying.

'Is it raining?' he asked, yawning and wondering how they were going to see lots of animals when it was still dark outside.

'No, though it did rain in the night,' Peter replied. 'I must have slept like a log because I didn't hear a thing.'

'You did sleep like a log – a snoring log,' said Joe. 'It poured last night.'

Peter picked up Joe's wet clothes from the floor. 'And it looks like someone couldn't resist going for a walk in it,' he said, chuckling.

'I was bursting to go to the loo, but I couldn't find the torch and got lost,' said Joe. 'I could have been wandering around for hours if I hadn't bumped into Kwame. You should have heard the jackals, Dad.'

'I heard the jackals too, and then I heard someone scream in the night,' said Aesha, who had appeared at the entrance to their tent. 'It was horrible.'

Joe blushed and asked her to leave so that he could get dressed.

'Mum says to hurry up. The cooks have made a pot of tea for us to drink before we go.'

Aesha and Peter left Joe to get ready. Joe remembered his conversation with Kwame.

'It had better be light soon and the ground

had better not be too wet,' he muttered to himself, grabbing a brown T-shirt and some camouflage trousers.

Daylight broke through very quickly and the sun was rising by the time the Brook family was on board the four-wheel-drive game-viewing truck that would take them into the heart of the reserve. Joe's spirits rose rapidly as they set off, especially when, within seconds, they spotted a herd of zebras grazing close to the track.

'Cool!' he cried. 'There must be at least twenty of them.'

He stood up on his seat with his head through the open roof, and lifted his camera. He took several photographs in quick succession, following his father's lead and using his long-distance lens to zoom in and out.

'Nice camera,' said Matunde, their guide.

Joe grinned. He had liked Matunde from the moment they were introduced, when the guide had done a high five with him and told him he was going to show him more animals than he could dream of.

'Look behind the zebras. What do you see?' Matunde was pointing now.

Joe stared hard but couldn't see anything else.

'It's some sort of antelope,' Aesha piped up.

'That's an eland,' said Matunde. 'The largest antelope in Africa.'

Joe spotted it just as Matunde drove on.

'In the tree – see? A fish eagle.'

Matunde slowed again to allow Peter and Joe to photograph it.

'It's beautiful!' Binti exclaimed.

'Look over there!' cried Aesha. 'Look at those tiny antelopes. They're so pretty.'

'Those are Thomson's gazelles,' said Matunde. 'We'll see lots of them.'

In a short space of time they had added wildebeests, baboons, storks and giraffes to the list of animals they had spotted. When Joe first caught sight of a giraffe stripping the branches of a tree, he could hardly contain his excitement, especially since Matunde left the track to allow them a closer look.

'He's amazing!' he cried. 'Look at his tongue!'

'That's a very prickly acacia tree he's eating from, yet his tongue is so tough that he doesn't feel a thing,' said Matunde.

They drove deeper into the reserve and for a while there were few animals in view, apart from more zebras and antelopes. Joe and Aesha competed with each other to see who could be the first to spot something, but more often than not Matunde beat them to it.

'When can we see a lion?' Joe asked him.

'Or an elephant?' said Aesha.

'Elephants coming up now, over there on the right,' Matunde answered, as though he had magicked them up to order.

A herd of seven elephants was foraging in the middle of a patch of low bushes. One of the elephants was huge and looked over to where

Matunde parked the safari van, its head swaying slightly from side to side. It took a step in the direction of the van, then stopped and watched.

'She's the matriarch and she's in charge,' Matunde said. 'She shows her family where to eat, what to do and how to survive. She has maybe forty years of experience to pass on.'

Joe stood on his seat again and lifted his camera through the open hatch in the top of the van. As he peered through the long-distance lens, a tiny calf appeared under the matriarch's belly, staying there for no more than twenty seconds before hiding among the other elephants.

'Did you see it?' he cried. 'Did you see the baby? I got a photo of it standing right underneath the big one.'

'You were quicker off the mark than me then,' said Peter. 'It had gone before I had time to focus.'

'I didn't see it at all,' said Aesha grumpily. 'You were in the way.'

They set off again, Binti noting that they had

now seen one of the Big Five and so had four to go.

'If your wish is to see the Big Five, then you will see the Big Five,' promised Matunde. 'I will do my very best.'

Part of their wish was granted almost immediately. Matunde left the track and drove through an area where the ground was very wet and covered with lush vegetation. He turned a corner and there, right in front of them, was a Cape buffalo, knee-deep in waterlogged undergrowth. The buffalo chewed slowly and fixed them with an unwavering stare.

'This is a very dangerous animal,' Matunde informed them. 'This is a very bad-tempered animal.'

'It looks it, too,' said Aesha.

Joe gazed at the buffalo's massive, curved horns before getting in position to take a photograph.

'Smile for the camera,' he said, and laughed as he clicked the shutter. 'That's two of the Big Five now, and I bet that one's the meanest.'

Matunde drove back on to the track, which took them through a long stretch of open savannah where again there was little to see except a few herds of zebras and wildebeests in the distance. The sun was much higher in the sky now and the day was heating up.

After a few kilometres, Matunde came to a halt, under the shade of a densely foliated tree, and encouraged them to get out of the van and have breakfast. Joe couldn't believe what he was telling them to do!

'But what if a lion comes?' he asked. 'Or a leopard?'

'It's perfectly safe,' Matunde said, grinning at him. 'It's too exposed for animals here, and I have my gun.'

Joe noticed for the first time that there was a shotgun next to the guide's seat.

I hope he doesn't have to use it, he thought. *I don't want him to kill anything.*

He soon forgot it, though, as he sat alongside Binti on a large rock under the tree, looking out over the endless expanse of wild grassland and breakfasting on generous hunks of bread and cheese, washed down with a bucket-load of chilled cola.

'Happy?' Binti asked him.

'Yes! This is the best!'

Chapter 8

The Brook family's safari resumed after breakfast and, to Joe's great joy, it wasn't long before they came across a large pride of lions with four young cubs.

'Look at them playing!' cried Aesha, as two of the cubs clambered on top of a resting male while the other two attacked his tail.

'They are learning how to kill,' said Matunde. 'Through play they learn how to stalk and attack and bring down their prey, like the females did with that zebra over there.'

It was only then that Joe spotted the remains of a carcass just beyond the romping cubs. The lions had obviously had their fill for the time being and were stretched out in the long grass, allowing their meal to settle.

'Gross!' muttered Aesha.

'Look up in that tree.' Matunde pointed. 'Two vultures are waiting to feast on what's left.'

Joe knew all about vultures from their trip to Ahmedabad in India, where his family had been involved in a conservation project.

'Are vultures endangered in Africa?' he asked.

'Their numbers are declining,' said Matunde. 'It's not good. They are needed to clean up what other animals leave, and that helps to stop the spread of disease.'

Binti asked him if anything was being done to halt their decline. While she was talking, Joe focused his attention back on to the lions and took numerous shots of the frolicking cubs, which were still pestering the sleepy male.

'He has the patience of a saint,' observed Peter, who was taking his own video footage.

At that very moment, the male cuffed one of the cubs and bowled it over.

'Not any more he doesn't.' Joe laughed.

They continued on their way and came across more giraffes and zebras, wildebeests and elephants, before Matunde informed them it was time to head back.

'It's getting too hot for many of the animals and they'll be finding shady places to sleep. We'll come back later in the day.'

Joe felt a pang of disappointment, because they still had two of the Big Five to see and as yet they hadn't come across any ostriches or cheetahs, either. But Matunde had promised they would see all five of the Big Five, so he had to hope that when they set out again in the late afternoon they would be able to put a tick against the leopard and the black rhino.

On returning to the campsite, they showered and freshened up before being taken by minibus to visit a nearby Maasai village.

'We think it's important for you to have an understanding of ways of life completely different from our own,' said Binti.

They had already seen some of the Maasai shepherds leading herds of goats and cattle on the edges of the reserve. Joe had been impressed by their long red tribal robes, their tightly cropped hair and by how tall and athletic-looking they were. Now, as they reached the village and were greeted by women and children who were decorated with colourful, intricately beaded jewellery and other adornments, he couldn't help staring at them in awe. When they were shown into a Maasai hut, which was a complex structure made of branches stuck together with mud, he found it difficult to believe that anyone could live in such a confined space, with so little light and so few possessions.

'How can anyone live with so few things?' whispered Aesha, echoing his thoughts.

'In many ways the simplicity of the Maasai way of life is enviable, especially because they're so in tune with the natural world,' said Binti. 'No university course can teach what tribes like the Maasai know through spending their lives immersed in nature. We've lost a lot by detaching ourselves more and more from our natural environment.'

'I couldn't live without a television and computers and stuff,' said Aesha. 'It would be so boring.'

Joe was inclined to agree, though he didn't say anything.

'I think I could be quite happy roaming the savannah and sitting outside my hut at the end of the day to watch the world go by with my family and friends,' said Peter.

'There's *nothing* going by!' Aesha scoffed.

'I bet there's more than you think,' replied Peter. 'We've just lost the knack of seeing it.'

'We're too accustomed to our own way of life to make such a radical change – even you, Peter Brook. You'd have ants in your pants in no time.' Binti smiled at him.

'He would, too, if he sat down there!' exclaimed Joe. 'There's a line of enormous ants!'

'Ah-ha!' said Peter. 'I told you there was a whole world going by.' He prepared his camera and knelt down to photograph them, Joe following suit.

'I don't see any Maasai people with cameras,' Aesha observed.

'I'd have to trade in my spear for one,' said Peter. 'Ouch – that hurts! One of those ants just bit me!'

'Ah,' said Binti. 'They obviously have a taste for plump pink flesh. That could be a problem if you were to live out here.'

Behind her, Joe noticed several of the Maasai girls giggling at his father's antics. He blushed, stood up and went to his mother's side.

'Shall we leave him here?' he whispered conspiratorially.

Chapter 9

Joe and his family snatched a couple of hours' sleep when they returned to the campsite. They were all tired from the early start to the day and the excitement of the safari. Joe thought it would be impossible even to doze in the daytime, especially since he couldn't wait to go back out on to the savannah, but he must have dropped off almost immediately and didn't have a clue where he was when Peter woke him again. He was upset to find that it had rained heavily while they were sleeping, and there was still some moisture in the air as they set off with Matunde for a second time.

'Rain makes it more interesting to go off-road,' Matunde said, grinning broadly.

'Does that mean we'll have to stick to the tracks?' Joe asked anxiously.

'We have leopards and rhinos to see,' said Matunde. 'If they don't come to us, we'll have to go to them!'

As the sun broke through the clouds and it began to heat up, water evaporated from the sodden ground, making it misty and difficult to see very far. Matunde and his group of eager travellers passed herds of zebras, several giraffes and even another pride of lions, all of which caused cries of delight, but none of which had quite the same impact as on first viewing. Joe was eager to spot an animal they hadn't seen before, and when he saw a strange, dark-grey shape, like an enormous swan on stilts, appearing through the mist, he held his breath in anticipation.

'Look!' he cried, when at last it became visible. 'An ostrich! It's enormous!'

The ostrich came closer, its head aloof, as though refusing to acknowledge its spectators, its long pink legs scything through the wet grass. Then, before Joe could pick up his camera, the ostrich began to lope away, its strides getting longer and longer, until it disappeared behind a line of trees.

'Cool!' said Joe, though he was dismayed he hadn't managed to take a photograph. 'They can run so fast!'

'Over seventy kilometres per hour,' said Matunde. 'It's one of the fastest creatures on earth.'

They continued for some distance without seeing anything else and Joe began to think that they would leave without spotting either a rhino or a leopard. He wasn't so worried about the rhino, because he knew he would soon be helping to release rhinos, though it wouldn't be the same as coming across one already living in the wild. But he was desperate to see a leopard. Matunde tried his best to locate both animals by liaising with other guides in the reserve via mobile phone, but the final two animals of the Big Five proved elusive.

'I have an idea where to go,' Matunde suddenly informed Joe and his family. 'Hold tight!'

He quickly left the track, heading towards an area in the distance where there was a greater density of trees and bushes and where the landscape looked more rugged.

Joe held on to the sides of his seat as the truck bounced up and down on the uneven ground. He began to feel exhilarated now that they had left the grassland and were ploughing through much thicker vegetation, turning this way and that to negotiate round rocks and other obstacles.

Wow! This is a real adventure!

He was delighted when they came across a troop of baboons and Matunde stopped to allow them to take photographs. Within minutes, the baboons were clambering all over the truck, peering through the windows and trying to find a way in. Aesha screamed when a large male tried to wriggle through the viewing gap at the top of the truck before Matunde had moved to close it, and then cooed when she saw that one of the baboons was carrying a baby.

'They're so funny!' cried Joe, as a young baboon stared at itself in a wing mirror and tried to groom its image.

Disaster struck when one of the baboons, encouraged by Matunde to take a piece of bread from his hand, leant through his open window and, quick as a flash, grabbed his mobile phone instead. The baboon jumped down from the truck, mobile in hand. Triumphant, it ran off with its prize, the rest of the troop scattering, as though fearful of repercussions.

Matunde shrugged. 'Now nobody knows where we are,' he said lightly, 'and nobody can tell us if they see a leopard. But it's not a worry. I will find one for you.'

Joe didn't know whether or not to believe him and thought he saw an anxious glance pass between his mother and his father.

Do they think we might not get to see a leopard now? Is it too late?

The sun was just beginning to set as Matunde turned the truck sharply across an area of scrub in the direction of a bank of tall trees. He had been particularly quiet during the past half hour, his eyes scouring every last scrap of land-scape, his ears alert to the slightest sounds. Something had obviously caught his attention, because he put his foot on the accelerator, taking the Brook family by surprise and throwing them sideways in their seats.

'Whoa, steady!' said Peter. 'Hold on, everyone.'

Joe could feel the wheels spinning on the wet undergrowth and the surge of the engine, straining to make them grip. The truck lurched forward and began to eat up the ground as Matunde urged it on – but the guide failed to see an overgrown ditch ahead. Seconds later, the truck had plunged into it, landing bonnet first against the far side, its rear bumper in the air.

Silence followed. It was as if the whole of the savannah was holding its breath in shock.

Chapter 10

'Are you all right, Joe? Aesha?' Binti's anxious voice broke through the silence.

Joe struggled to his feet from the floor of the truck. 'I think so,' he said. He felt something wet and warm trickle down his face and touched it with his hand. 'I've cut my forehead,' he added, 'but it's nothing much.'

'I banged my knee.' Aesha groaned. 'What happened?'

'We've skidded into a ditch.' Peter's head appeared over the back of his seat. 'No broken bones?'

'Matunde isn't moving.' Binti leant over the

70

driver's seat, from where Matunde had been thrown forward – he was now prostrate over the steering wheel. The glass of the windscreen had shattered and there was a gaping hole in it.

Peter climbed over the back of the passenger seat into the cab and checked Matunde's pulse.

'His pulse is fine,' he reported. 'It looks as if he knocked himself unconscious on the steering wheel – there's a big bump on his forehead.'

Peter wound down a window and looked out. 'The ditch isn't deep, but I'm not sure how we're going to get the truck out. It's wedged nose-down at an angle of forty-five degrees and the back wheels are in the air.'

Binti opened a bottle of water, tipped some on to a small bandanna she had brought with her and handed the bandanna to Peter. He tried to lift Matunde away from the steering wheel in order to apply it to his forehead, but it was difficult because of the angle of the truck. Instead, he tried to revive him by holding the bandanna against the guide's neck, reapplying fresh water when it became too warm. Meanwhile, Binti saw to the cut on Joe's forehead with a plaster she found in a first-aid tin that was stowed in the pocket of the truck door.

'Will Matunde be all right?' Joe asked.

'I'm sure he will,' Binti replied. 'He must have taken quite a bump, though.'

'How are we going to get out of here?' Aesha asked the other question that was playing on Joe's mind.

'That's a bit of a conundrum,' said Peter.

He turned to smile at them, but Joe could tell he was troubled. The light was fading fast and, as far as they knew, they were a long way from anywhere.

'We can't even phone anyone because of those stupid baboons,' Aesha grumbled.

Joe stared at her. *Nobody knows where we are!*

In the driver's seat, Matunde stirred and muttered something incomprehensible, before falling silent again.

'When he comes to, we'll have a go at seeing if we can shift the truck,' said Peter, though he sounded extremely doubtful. 'If we all get out and push —'

'Looking at the angle of the truck,' said Binti, 'I don't think there's even the remotest chance we'll be able to shift it.'

'And I don't want to get out,' Aesha added. 'What if an animal spots us?'

Joe shivered. He was glad his parents were with them. He had wanted an African adventure, but this was turning out to be more than a little scary.

How long will we have to stay here? he wondered. *We can't even sit properly without sliding off the seats.*

The only way he could stay in his seat was to put both feet against the seat in front, so that he was half-sitting, half-standing. Aesha had done the same, though she complained that it hurt her knee. Binti and Peter were half-standing up and half-leaning against the driver and front passenger seats, both of them deep in thought.

They don't know what to do! realised Joe. *They always know what to do, but they don't know what to do now!*

Joe was shocked to grasp that for once his parents were powerless to make things happen.

Matunde stirred again. Peter applied the damp compress to his neck and reached forward to wipe his face.

'I hope he's all right,' said Binti.

'It's his fault we're in this mess,' Aesha complained. 'We should never have let him take us away from the tracks.'

'We can't blame him for doing his best for us,' Peter replied. 'He knew how much we wanted –'

'Dad! Look behind you, Dad!'

The urgency in Joe's voice and the fear in his eyes made Peter stop what he was saying and spin round.

'Where?' he asked.

'Just behind that boulder.'

Joe pointed through the windscreen. Just visible above a large boulder was the head of a rhino, its eyes focused on the truck with its stranded passengers.

Chapter 11

'Let's just keep calm,' said Peter. 'We're safe in here.'

'What about the hole in the windscreen?' Binti pointed out.

'The ditch will protect us from an attack from the front,' Peter replied.

'I thought black rhinos were supposed to be rare,' Aesha whispered. 'I can't believe one has appeared just when we least want to see it!'

They stared back out at the rhino, which flicked its ear to remove an irritating fly but continued to gaze in their direction.

I wanted to see a rhino in the wild, thought Joe, *but not like this.*

'It looks awesome with the sun setting in the background,' Peter observed, picking up his camera.

'Surely you're not going to take a photo when we're in danger of being crushed!' protested Aesha.

'It's my job,' Peter said simply.

He bent down, put his arm round the side of the driver's seat and picked up Matunde's shotgun.

'I'll only use it if I have to,' he added, seeing Joe's consternation.

Joe hardly dared pick up his own camera, but it was too good an opportunity to miss.

Imagine what my friends will say when I show them the photo and tell them the rhino could have attacked us!

The rhino seemed quite happy to stand behind the boulder and pose while Joe and his father took one photograph after another. Binti and Aesha watched anxiously for any sign that it was developing anything more than a passing interest in its audience. When it took a few steps towards them, Aesha let out a scream, but it stopped, turned away from them and disappeared into some bushes.

'Thank goodness for that.' Binti sighed, after waiting for a few moments to see if it was going to reappear. 'I might be used to dealing with large animals, but I prefer it to be on my terms.'

The night was closing in fast when Matunde finally began to move again. He leant back awkwardly in his seat, swaying precariously, and tried to work out where he was.

'What happened?' he asked when Peter put a hand on his shoulder and told him everything was all right.

'We seem to have landed in a ditch and we can't get out of it,' said Peter.

'It's my fault.' Matunde shook his head. 'It

was too wet, but I wanted to find you a rhino and I know one lives here.'

'We've seen it!' piped up Joe. 'It was behind that boulder there. We got some amazing photos!'

Matunde pulled a torch from under the dashboard and switched it on, but then thought better of it and switched it off again.

'I need to see if the truck will move,' he muttered.

He turned the key in the ignition, but Peter restrained him.

'The truck's not going anywhere,' he said. 'We need someone to come and rescue us.'

He didn't have time to say any more. There was a loud bang and the truck shook. Aesha yelped. Joe held his breath. Peter took hold of the shotgun. Matunde tried to grab it from him, but Peter refused to let go.

'You're still concussed,' he hissed. 'It's better if I have it.'

'Hold on tight to the seats and keep together

in the middle of the truck,' Binti told Joe and Aesha, as it shook again.

'It's the rhino!' Joe whispered. 'It's barging us from behind the truck.'

'Shhh!' Binti warned him.

'What if it tips the truck over?' Aesha was terrified.

'It won't,' Peter said firmly.

They could hear the rhino snorting and the thump of its feet on the ground. There was another violent bang, and Joe lost his grip. He fell sideways on to Aesha, who lost her balance and landed in the well of the truck with Joe on top of her.

'Mum told you to hold on,' Aesha hissed, as he grappled to stand up.

'Keep quiet,' Peter warned them.

Minutes passed by, with no one daring to move. Darkness settled around them, the last glowing cinders of the magnificent sunset extinguished by clouds and a fresh shower of rain dampening the air. The only light came from the intermittent rays of a three-quarter moon. Joe shivered as a chill wind blew through the broken windscreen.

Something dark rammed the side of the truck. Aesha screamed. Matunde shouted. In a brief burst of moonlight, Joe saw the rhino's face, tiny eyes staring, horn poised, ready to charge. He felt for his mother's hand and Binti squeezed his hand in return.

A loud bang ripped through the night, followed by another and another. Joe winced.

Don't kill it! Please don't kill it . . .

'He's gone.' Matunde spoke first. 'That frightened him off. Shoot again to let the rangers know where we are. They'll have noticed by now that we haven't returned to the campsite.'

Joe put his fingers in his ears as his father fired several more shots, this time leaning out through an open window and aiming the rifle upward.

'I don't think he'll be back,' said Peter. 'I

think he'll decide there are better ways to spend the night.'

'Let's hope the rangers find us before something else comes along,' said Binti.

Chapter 12

It was another half an hour before the Brook family's exact whereabouts were discovered. A park ranger arrived in a four-wheel drive and took them back to their campsite, while calling for reinforcements to ferry Matunde to a clinic for a check-up and to pull his truck from the ditch in the morning.

'Well, we managed to see four of the Big Five,' said Peter, as they sat around the camp-fire after their evening meal. 'I hope that was enough of an adventure for you, Joe.'

'I was terrified!' Aesha butted in. 'That rhino was determined to make mincemeat of us.'

'I thought you'd shot it when the gun went off, Dad,' said Joe. 'I'm so glad you didn't. Aren't you, Mum?'

Binti nodded, adding, 'But if it had been a choice between us and the rhino, I'm afraid I would have told your father to shoot the rhino.'

'Too right!' said Aesha.

'I wish we'd seen a leopard in the wild, though,' said Joe.

Exhaustion was taking hold and they returned to their tents.

Joe fell asleep with the face of the rhino staring at him, and woke the next morning from a dream where a rhino was about to charge at their car back home in England. He thought it was still early and lay for a moment, listening to the sound of birdsong and the occasional human voice, until he looked across to his father's bed and saw that it was empty. He jumped up, dressed and hurried to find his family.

Binti and Peter were sitting in the sun,

drinking coffee and eating pastries. There was no sign of Aesha, but Matunde was leaning against the wall of the eating area, a huge bump in the middle of his forehead. As soon as he saw the plaster on Joe's forehead, he did a high five with him, apologised for the accident and said he was feeling just fine.

'The truck is not so fine,' he admitted.

'When you said you would find us a rhino,' said Joe, 'I didn't realise we were going to see one quite so close!'

'I try my best for my customers,' Matunde replied, grinning. 'You're very lucky, because now you're off to help in the release of rhinos.'

'And to take photos,' said Joe, looking at Peter.

'I don't think any photo we take from now on will be as exciting as the ones we took last night,' Peter remarked.

'Unless the rhinos stampede,' replied Joe. 'That would be cool!'

'Don't!' interjected Aesha, who had just

joined them. 'We've had enough drama for one trip.'

Shortly afterwards, a minibus arrived to take them to Tsavo West, another game reserve. Joe was sorry to have to say goodbye to Matunde, and wished their guide could go with them. Matunde shook hands with him and slipped a bangle over his wrist.

'Come back one day,' he said, 'and I will find you a leopard.'

He gave a beaded necklace to Aesha, and promised Peter and Binti that if they returned he would introduce them to his family and cook them a traditional Maasai meal.

'How could we possibly resist?' Binti smiled. 'It would be an honour.'

They clambered into the minibus and turned to wave. As they left the Maasai Mara behind they were quiet for a while, all of them occupied with their own thoughts, until Peter began to talk about the project they would soon be involved with.

'The rhinos live in a secure fenced community,' he explained. 'Ten of them are to be set free, each one into a different area of Tsavo West. We'll only be able to watch one of the releases, so there'll be no mass stampede.'

He saw Joe's face drop.

'But there'll still be plenty to photograph – you'll see Mount Kilimanjaro on the horizon, and Tsavo West has lots of hippos and crocodiles.'

Joe's face lit up again at the mention of hippos and crocodiles. He had forgotten all about them being on his list of animals he wanted to see.

'Does that mean we're going on safari again?' he asked excitedly.

'We certainly are,' said Peter. 'Not only that, but this time we'll be able to leave our vehicle and wander round Mzima Springs, where we can get up close and personal with both crocodiles and hippos.'

'Not me!' cried Aesha. 'You won't catch me going near them.'

'It's safe enough,' Peter replied. 'They're much happier wallowing in the springs than chasing after landlubbers like us. Unless you're thinking of going for a swim.'

'Funny, ha, ha, Dad,' Aesha retorted.

'One day with a rhino, one day with hippos and crocodiles, then off to Tanzania to relax with my family,' said Binti. 'I think we'll need it by then.'

Joe settled back in his seat. It was a long journey from the Maasai Mara to Tsavo West and would take the rest of the day. He was looking forward to arriving at the reserve, where they were going to stay at a lodge rather than a campsite, and where the toilets were inside. His walk in the middle of the night and the fright he had had on bumping into the Maasai patrolman seemed such a long time ago. *So much has happened since then!*

Joe slept most of the way. On arrival at the lodge, he and Aesha were thrilled to discover that their parents had been keeping a secret from them. Only when they sat down to dinner and looked out at the brightly lit gardens did they see that there was a waterhole close by. Moreover, a herd of elephants was splashing around in it, the older ones spraying the youngsters with water, while a short distance behind them two giraffes awaited their turn.

'This trip just gets better and better!' exclaimed Joe.

Chapter 13

Joe could barely sleep for thinking about the wildlife just outside and kept going to the bedroom window to see what was there. In the course of the night he saw zebras and monkeys, gazelles and a group of motley hyenas.

In the morning he leapt out of bed to find an elephant and calf drinking at the waterhole, the sun shining brightly behind them. He fetched his camera and took several shots of them, hoping he might have caught something on film that his father had missed.

He found his parents on the viewing deck,

talking to a young man with long hair, dressed in shorts and a T-shirt.

'Ah, Joe,' said Binti. 'This is Jack White from the United States. He's been telling us about his research work with the rhinos in the reserve.'

'That's right,' said Jack. 'I'm here as a volunteer for six weeks, monitoring their movements, checking where they feed, sleep, defecate – everything about them. Staying in this lodge for a night is a bonus – I can stretch my legs out! Mostly I've been sleeping in a teeny-tiny tent in the middle of the reserve.'

'Jack's coming with us today as part of his project,' said Peter. 'And he'll be tracking the rhino that's being released.'

'Have you told him about the rhino that attacked us?' Joe asked.

'Yes, that must have been mighty scary,' Jack said, nodding. 'Rhinos like nothing better than a sitting target to charge at.'

After breakfast and while they waited for their guide to arrive, Jack sat at their table and showed them some of the photographs he had taken in the reserve. Joe was delighted when they came to one of a rhino calf.

'He's just like Rombo, the orphan rhino we've adopted,' he explained.

'This little guy was romping around and biffing everything in sight.' Jack laughed. 'Including his poor mother and a passing warthog!'

The most dramatic photograph was of a huge male rhino galloping towards the camera and throwing up a whirlwind of dust.

'That was a dodgy moment.' Jack grimaced. 'I only just got out of the way in time!'

'I think you should call the photo "Danger in the Dust",' suggested Joe.

Peter chuckled. 'You can see my son is taking after his father with naming his photos,' he said.

A few minutes later, a guide arrived in a four-by-four to take them to the location in the reserve where one of the rhinos was to be released. Joe insisted on sitting next to Jack. He wanted to ask him what it was like to sleep in a tent in the middle of the reserve. He was sure it must be terrifying, especially after the fright he had had. However, Jack said it was the best experience in the world and that listening to the sounds of the night was awesome and more than made up for any discomfort or fear.

It wasn't too long before they reached the agreed meeting point. The lorry carrying the rhino had yet to arrive, which gave the Brook family time to stare in wonder at Mount Kilimanjaro, with its frozen peak.

'My country is just over the other side of that mountain,' Binti said wistfully. 'I can't wait to be there.'

Joe gave her a hug. 'You will be soon, Mum,' he said.

'I'll be going there in a few months' time to work with elephants in the Serengeti National Park,' said Jack.

'Then you must call on my family,' said Binti. 'They'll make you very welcome.'

A prolonged low rumble announced the arrival of a lorry, on the back of which was a huge metal crate. Joe felt his heart skip a beat. This was the main purpose of their trip and he wasn't going to miss a moment of it. The lorry moved slowly towards them and stopped a short distance ahead, turning round so that it faced them. It was followed by a truck, which parked to the side and a little way behind it. As soon as the truck came to a halt, half a dozen men jumped out and shook hands with everyone. One of them introduced himself as Rajesh, the senior conservation biologist in charge of the rehabilitation project.

'We have a rather perplexed and angry rhino in that crate – the effects of the sedation have nearly worn off,' he observed.

'Is it a male or a female?' Joe asked.

'Her name's Harriet,' Rajesh replied. 'And the sooner we get her out the better, but first we need to make some preparations.' He looked from Joe to Aesha. 'I need you to stand well clear for the time being, but I might have a little job for you when we're ready. Would you like to help?'

Joe nodded eagerly. He couldn't wait to be part of what was about to happen. Aesha, less certain, nodded too.

Binti took them to sit inside the truck, while Peter stood beside it and set up his filming equipment and camera. Jack climbed into the back of the truck and started making notes.

'I'll get a chance to take some photos as well, won't I, Mum?' Joe asked, suddenly anxious that he wouldn't be able to make the most of the opportunity.

'I'm sure you will,' Binti reassured him. 'Just wait and see.'

Joe peered through the windscreen of the truck as two of the men fixed a ramp to the back of the lorry, the clang of metal against metal a violent intrusion of the peaceful natural surroundings. There was a loud bang from inside the crate.

'Harriet's making her feelings known,' said Joe.

'She sounds hopping mad, and I don't blame her.' Aesha pouted.

'But in a few minutes, she'll be as free as a bird,' said Binti.

The two men carefully unlatched the crate as two others joined them. One shouted a signal to the rest, and together they pulled at the heavy doors until they were wide open. The men ran for cover.

Everyone watched with bated breath. Joe fully expected the rhino to come charging out and disappear into the distance, never to be seen again. Instead, nothing happened for what seemed like minutes on end.

Then, little by little, Harriet's head appeared.

'Here she comes!' Joe could scarcely contain his excitement.

The rhino stepped cautiously on to the ramp and stood as though waiting for instructions. Just then, Joe spotted Rajesh holding up a rifle and aiming it towards Harriet.

'What's he doing?' Joe cried.

'He's going to fire a tranquilliser dart to stop her running off,' Binti explained.

'But isn't that what they want her to do?' asked Aesha.

'They need to make sure she's calm and that she goes in the right direction,' said Binti.

Harriet began to move forward, crashing her feet on the metal ramp, as though beating out a warning. Rajesh opened fire and buried a dart in the animal's rump. The rhino continued forward. Her front feet left the ramp and found the softness of grass. In another couple of steps, she had cleared the ramp completely. She began to sway, her huge body rocking precariously. The men ran out from behind the lorry, surrounded her and carefully lowered her to the ground.

Chapter 14

The moment Rajesh signalled that it was safe, everyone sprang into action. Two men closed the crate and drove the lorry behind a patch of dense vegetation so that it was scarcely visible. Another man followed with the truck. Peter picked up his photographic equipment and moved closer to the sedated rhino.

Rajesh crouched down beside her and beckoned to Joe and Aesha.

'Come,' he said. 'Let me introduce you to Harriet.'

Aesha, Joe and Binti jumped down from the

truck. They hurried over to the rhino and knelt next to her.

'Wow!' said Joe. 'She's amazing!'

Jack knelt down with them, while Rajesh monitored her heartbeat and then allowed Binti to check it as well.

'She's the most incredible creature, isn't she?' Jack said. 'She certainly wouldn't have looked out of place at the time of the dinosaurs.'

'She's extraordinary,' said Binti.

Joe studied her wrinkled browny-grey hide, her fat stumpy legs and short tail. Rajesh pointed to a patch of skin that was mottled and bumpy.

'This is caused by parasites like ticks,' he explained. 'Oxpecker birds do a great job of cleaning them off, but it's a never-ending battle.'

Aesha could hardly bring herself to watch, but Joe stared intently as Rajesh pinched out several ticks and scrubbed the mottled skin with a stiff brush.

'We want Harriet to look her best, don't we?' Rajesh grinned.

Joe picked up his camera and took several photographs of her.

And I thought I wouldn't be taking close-up shots of a rhino!

'We haven't got long now,' said Rajesh, getting to his feet. 'When Harriet wakes up she needs to feel at home, so are you ready to help?'

Joe and Aesha nodded.

'We've removed all distractions, and now there's something else we need to do,' Rajesh continued.

He walked over to one of the men, who was holding four buckets. He took two of the buckets and returned with them to a puzzled-looking Joe and Aesha.

'Would you like to spread this around for me? It will reassure Harriet that there are other rhinos in the vicinity.'

Rajesh waited for their reaction. The buckets were full of rhino dung.

Joe chuckled. 'It won't be the first time we've had to deal with poo,' he said, remembering when he and Aesha had helped train dogs to identify tiger scat in eastern Russia.

Aesha pulled a face. 'I'm glad I don't need to be surrounded by dung to feel at home,' she remarked as, rather disgustedly, she took hold of a bucket.

'Just general mess in your case,' said Peter, taking a quick photograph of them as they stood there with their buckets.

'You're not funny, Dad,' Aesha replied scornfully.

Rajesh told them exactly what he wanted them to do, asked them to be quick and then knelt down with Harriet to check her pulse again.

Aesha set about tipping small piles of dung next to the rhino. Joe, feeling important despite the job he had been tasked with, laid a trail leading towards the reserve, helped by Jack and one of the other men.

'I've done a lot of strange things in my life,' Jack said, 'but this one takes some beating.'

'I bet you haven't put your arm up a cow's bottom like Mum has to,' Joe said, tipping out the last of the dung.

'No, and I think I'll pass on that.' Jack laughed. 'All done here,' he called back to Rajesh.

'Good job,' Rajesh replied. 'It's nearly time to bring Harriet round, so all of you need to move well out of sight.'

The Brook family and Jack hurried to where the truck was parked and climbed into the back of it. Peter clambered on to the roof with his equipment, and prepared to take a video of Harriet's escape to freedom.

From their cover, Joe watched as Rajesh leant over the comatose rhino and administered an antidote to the tranquilliser. The rest of the men stood by, ready to act as soon as she made any sign of movement.

Harriet's ears twitched first, and then one of her legs shook. Rajesh laid a cloth over her face, which Binti explained to Aesha and Joe was to prevent her from trying to bolt the minute she was upright.

'If she can't see, she'll stay still,' Binti said.

Aided by the men, the rhino climbed unsteadily to her feet, at which point they fled into the bushes, leaving Rajesh on his own. As soon as everyone was hidden, the biologist pulled the cloth from Harriet's face and walked backwards away from her.

Harriet gazed uncertainly at the unfamiliar world that opened up in front of her, her tiny eyes trying to find their focus, her ears swivelling to and fro.

'The poor thing is wondering where on earth she is,' whispered Aesha.

'Can you imagine being dumped in the middle of nowhere, waking up as if from a dream and finding yourself completely on your own?' said Jack.

'I hope she'll learn to love her new home and thrive here,' said Rajesh, coming over to join them.

After a few moments, Harriet seemed to catch the scent of a pile of rhino droppings. She plodded over, lowered her head towards them, and then trotted on to another pile and another.

'She's going in the right direction,' whispered Joe. 'She's following our poo trail!'

'She's grazing on some grass now,' said Rajesh. 'That's a good sign. She wouldn't be doing that if she wasn't relaxed.'

Joe was delighted at the part he had played in Harriet's release. He linked arms with his mother. 'We've had the most amazing rhino adventures, haven't we, Mum?'

Chapter 15

They continued to watch Harriet for well over an hour. She took her time, checking out every last fraction of the area around the trail of dung, sniffing at the vegetation and foraging among the branches of low trees. With every step, she moved further away from her spectators and deeper into the park.

And then, suddenly, without any warning, she bolted. One minute she was eating, the next she was off, almost as if something had frightened her and she couldn't wait to get away from it. The last they saw of her was her ample rump disappearing through a dense row of bushes.

'That's a great last photo I've just taken,' Peter said, smiling.

'Let's hope Harriet meets the rhino of her dreams, produces healthy offspring and lives to a ripe old age,' said Binti.

'You're such a romantic.' Peter laughed.

'Poachers had better not find her,' said Joe.

'She's got the best of chances,' said Rajesh. 'And tomorrow it will be Kojo's turn to run free, but in a different part of the reserve.'

Joe wished he could be there too, as they said their goodbyes to Jack and Rajesh and his team, until he remembered that his family was going to Mzima Springs to see the crocodiles and hippos.

I can't believe how many different things we've done and places we've been and animals we've seen already, and the trip isn't over yet!

Back at the lodge that evening, the Brook family reflected upon their experiences while they watched the animals coming and going from the waterhole.

'This beats television, don't you think?' said Peter.

'I can't stop looking around,' said Joe. 'You just never know what's going to arrive next.'

'I'm half-expecting a rhino to appear,' said Aesha.

'As long as it's not Harriet!' Joe exclaimed.

'If she does appear, she'll definitely take the prize for being the fastest animal on earth!' Binti laughed.

'Rhinos are surprisingly quick for such a large animal,' said Peter. 'Our Harriet galloped off like a racehorse!'

'I wonder what will happen to our Rombo,' said Joe. 'I can't wait to read the first newsletter about him. I hope he can be rehabilitated eventually, too.'

'Will we be able to visit him again before he leaves the orphanage?' Aesha asked.

Binti smiled at her. 'Have you changed your mind about rhinos?'

Aesha shrugged. 'I still think they look

grumpy,' she said, 'and I never want to be attacked by one again, but they're sort of beautiful in their own way, and there's nothing else like them.'

'A bit like my daughter, then.' Peter chuckled, which earned a snort of disdain from Aesha.

All of a sudden Joe remembered that they hadn't seen a leopard. He stared at the waterhole, willing one to appear.

'We haven't seen a leopard,' he said, voicing his disappointment. 'Do you think we might tomorrow?'

'Who knows?' said Binti. 'That's what's so marvellous about being here. It's gloriously unpredictable and that's how life in the wild should be. It's easy to forget that the animals out there are fighting for their survival. Nobody is standing round the corner with a bag of goodies to feed them with, and if they don't show up to order then that's what makes it all the more exciting when they do appear.'

'If you look round now,' Peter added, 'you

might not see a leopard, but there's something very special heading in your direction.'

Joe spun round to see a vervet monkey scooting along the balcony towards him. Before he knew what was happening, the monkey snatched a piece of bread from his plate and ran off, shrieking triumphantly.

'You see what I mean?' Binti laughed. 'It's gloriously unpredictable, and we've been very, very lucky to see what we've seen.'

Joe nodded. 'And there's still more to come.'

Zoological Society of London

ZSL London Zoo is a very famous part of the
Zoological Society of London (ZSL).

For almost two hundred years, we have been
working tirelessly to provide hope and a
home to thousands of animals.

And it's not just the animals at ZSL's Zoos in
London and Whipsnade that we are caring for.
Our conservationists are working in more than
50 countries to help protect animals in the wild.

In Nepal and Kenya we are fighting to protect the
highly threatened greater one-horned and black
rhinos through vital conservation projects.

But all of this wouldn't be possible without your help.
As a charity we rely entirely on the generosity of our
supporters to continue this vital work.

By buying this book, you have made an essential
contribution to help protect animals.
Thank you.

Find out more at **zsl.org**

Turn the page for a taster of Joe's exciting adventures at an Indian kite festival in

Feathers in the Wind

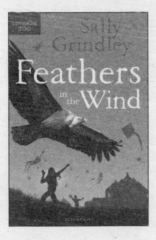

The annual kite festival fills the Indian city of Ahmedabad with bright colours and fierce competition, but the kites have a devastating side effect on the bird population.

As the skies come alive, Joe and Aesha put themselves at risk to protect a magnificent vulture . . .

Chapter 1

'Vultures!' Aesha pulled a face. 'Why would we go all the way to India to hang out with vultures? They're ugly and disgusting.' She pushed her dinner plate away as though it contained something distasteful.

'They speak very highly of you too,' her father, Peter, replied.

'I think they're rather handsome,' said her mother. 'And they fulfil a very vital role.'

'Like scavenging on things that other animals have killed,' Aesha said scornfully.

'That's exactly right,' said Binti. 'They clean up what's been left, and that's very important in helping to prevent disease. Talking of which, it's your turn to clear the table.'

'What's India like?' Joe asked.

Their mother, Binti, who was an international vet, had just announced that they were going to spend time there while she helped with research into why vulture numbers were declining to such an extent that they were becoming endangered.

'It's hot and noisy and chaotic and full of wonderful smells and there's an amazing photo to be taken every few seconds,' Peter told him.

Joe perked up at the idea of that. He had his very own camera and wanted to follow in his father's footsteps as a wildlife photographer.

'So why are vultures in India endangered?' Aesha wanted to know. 'We saw lots of them when we were in Africa.'

'It seems they may be sensitive to a drug used to treat cattle,' Binti replied.

'Vultures don't eat cattle, do they?' said Joe.

'Yes, they do,' said Binti. 'When cattle die,

farmers take their carcasses to a communal place and leave them for vultures and other scavengers to pick over. Traces of the drug have been found in some carcasses, and there appears to be a link between that and the dramatic reduction in vulture numbers.'

'So they need to stop using the drug,' said Aesha. 'Job done.' She pushed back her chair and collected the dirty plates.

'If only it were that simple,' said Binti. 'Farmers rely on certain drugs to keep their cattle healthy. And cattle are vital to the farmers' livelihoods.'

'It's never simple, is it, Mum?' Joe commented.

Foggy the dog woke from his slumber under the table and nestled his head on Joe's knee.

'So many things depend on other things, don't they, Foggy?' he continued.

'Upset one cog in a finely tuned engine and the whole lot grinds to a halt,' his father agreed. 'It's the same with the natural world, and it's usually man's interference that causes the problem.'

'Sometimes human beings are so dumb. We do so much damage to the world around us.' Aesha sounded as if she'd rather not be human. Joe often wondered if she was an alien rather than his sister.

'Sometimes a perfectly innocent pursuit can cause problems,' said Binti. 'One of the things that's not helping the vulture population in India is kite-flying. That's the main reason for my trip.'

'Kite-flying!' Joe was incredulous. 'How can kite-flying affect vultures?'

'It probably scares them!' said Aesha.

'It's worse than that. January the fourteenth is the annual International Kite Festival in Ahmedabad, where we're staying. Everyone flies kites to celebrate Uttarayan – the end of winter and beginning of summer,' Binti explained. 'They cover the strings of the kites with ground glass, which makes them sharp.

The idea is that kite-flyers target rival kites and try to cut them out of the sky. Sadly, large numbers of vultures get caught up in the strings.'

Joe grimaced at the thought of what could happen to the vultures.

'Mum, that's awful!' Aesha cried. 'Surely not many vultures would fly into them, would they?'

'Yes, unfortunately – especially since the festival covers such a huge area,' said Peter. 'Your mother will be helping to save the injured birds while we're there.'

Joe looked at his mother with pride. Not only did his mother come from Tanzania, which meant he was half-African, but he and Aesha were lucky enough to travel the world because of their parents' professions. *It's so cool having an international vet for a mum*, he thought.

Chapter 2

The next few days passed in a whirl as Joe and his family prepared themselves for their trip. Joe was excited about all the opportunities he would have to take photographs, and the more he thought about the kite festival, the more he wanted his own kite to fly.

'I wouldn't want to put glass on the string because of the vultures, but it would be so cool to fly a kite with everyone else,' he said to his mother and father, hoping they would agree and buy him one.

They arrived at the boarding kennels and said their goodbyes to Foggy, who trotted off happily enough as soon as he spotted another dog in the distance.

Their last stop was Peter's favourite photographic shop, where he stocked up on equipment to take the amazing wildlife photographs that hung on the walls of their house and appeared in newspapers and magazines. Joe gazed enthusiastically at the cabinets and shelves with their displays of cameras in all shapes and sizes, as well as lenses and leads, cases and batteries. There was so much more to taking a photograph than pointing a camera and pressing a button.

As they left the shop, Peter handed Joe a small package. 'It's a zoom lens for your camera,' he said. 'You'll need it for photographing those kites . . .'

OUT NOW

Don't miss Joe's thrilling animal adventures across the world!

Join Joe as he helps to look after endangered tigers in Russia, seahorses in the Philippines, vultures in India and rhinos in Kenya . . .

OUT NOW